MR. MEN   LITTLE MISS

MR. MEN™ LITTLE MISS™ © THOIP (a SANRIO company)

Mr. Men My Mummy © 2017 THOIP (a SANRIO company)
Printed and published under licence from Price Stern Sloan, Inc., Los Angeles.
Published in Great Britain by Egmont UK Limited
The Yellow Building, 1 Nicholas Road, London, W11 4AN

ISBN 978 1 4052 8550 6
66494/1
Printed in Italy

MIX
Paper from
responsible sources
FSC® C018306

FSC
www.fsc.org

MY MUMMY

by Roger Hargreaves

and me

My mummy brightens my day from the moment she wakes up.

She is like Little Miss Sunshine on a cloudy day.

My mummy can do more than one thing at a time, like magic.

And when she reads me stories, I feel like I'm really there.

My mummy is very friendly and likes to talk a lot.

But she is also very good at listening, especially to me.

My mummy is very curious and sometimes asks lots of questions.

But she is also very wise and knows lots of answers.

My mummy knows when I am hungry.

And when I am tired.

My mummy can be very silly and always makes me smile.

She gives the best hugs
and knows just when they
are needed.

My mummy has
a splendid sense
of style.

And she has lots of interesting things stored in mysterious boxes.

My mummy loves eating cake, just like me.

And sometimes she needs time to herself, too.

My mummy can be a bit cheeky.

But she is always kind.

My mummy is lots of fun
and loves birthday parties.

She is really good at playing games like hide-and-seek.

And my mummy is a brilliant dancer, too.

Even when things go wrong, my mummy makes me smile.

When she giggles, it makes me giggle too.

And when I make my mummy happy, she jumps for joy!

There is no one like my mummy, though sometimes I wish there were two of her.

My mummy is SO very special. My mummy loves me, and I love my mummy.

MY MUMMY

My mummy is most like **LITTLE MISS** ....

I love it when my mummy reads ....

.... to me.

My mummy makes me laugh when...

....

She always knows when..

....

My mummy is very kind because ....

....

My mummy is lots of fun and likes ....

Her favourite game to play with me is ....

I know she loves me when ....

My mummy's hugs are the best because ....

....

This is a picture
of my mummy:

by ....

aged ....